Marge
in
Charge

AND THE
STOLEN TREASURE

Marge
in
Charge

AND THE
STOLEN TREASURE

ISLA FISHER

Illustrated by Eglantine Ceulemans

HARPER

An Imprint of HarperCollinsPublishers

www.harpercollinschildrens.com

ISBN 978-0-06-266222-4

18 19 20 21 22 BRR 10 9 8 7 6 5 4 3 2 1

First U.S. paperback edition, 2019
Originally published in the U.K. by Picadilly Press
under the title *Marge and the Pirate Baby*

For Olive, Elula, and Monty.
My favorite small people on the planet
and the best editors a writer could wish for.

And to my mom and dad, who are more fun
than any wacky babysitter.

the Button Family

Mommy

Dad

Jake

Me
(Jemima)

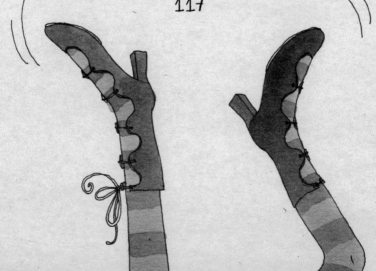

Marge the Pirate Nanny

Hello again—it's me, Jemima Button. I'm back. I am so excited for today because Marge, our extraordinary babysitter, is coming over. We used to be an ordinary family until she came along. I know what you're thinking—babysitters are boring—but you haven't met Marge. Incredible things happen whenever Marge is around. Like the time she led our entire school in an outdoor concert with her head stuck in a tuba. Or the time she wanted to tie balloons to Jakey's feet to see if he would float to school.

Jakeypants is still my little brother, even though sometimes I wish he wasn't. And he still loves wrestling and dinosaurs, but now he also loves pirates—a lot. At the moment, he's sitting next to me on a blanket in the backyard, building a pirate ship out of Legos.

The only bad part is that our cousin baby Zara will be here later.

I am trying to keep my mind off that by drawing a self-portrait (which is a picture of myself) to show Marge. I am the second best drawer in my class after Emily Fox, who can draw fingers and toes perfectly.

We haven't seen Zara for a while (thank goodness), and apparently now she can crawl. When she was first born, she was a bald blob with eyelashes and she couldn't do much at all. Mommy says that I looked exactly the same when I was small and that we could be sisters! But we are definitely not sisters because Zara is very naughty. No one believes Jakey and me when we say that even though Zara looks like an angel, she is definitely not one. I have written in my secret diary a list of all the bad things that she has done to me:

1. DRAWING all over my library book

2. SQUEEZING toothpaste into my doll house

3. PULLING the head off my Beach Barbie

Would you believe that I couldn't find my Barbie's head anywhere? Then the next time Dad turned on the oven, there was a horrible smell and out came a hairy, yellow alien.

Still, I have lined up all my dollies in a row by the front door to welcome Zara today. Except for Sarah, my Cabbage Patch doll. I cut Sarah's hair short and now she looks scary. I don't want her to frighten my little cousin, because when Zara cries it's so loud I have to put my fingers in my ears. Last time we saw her, Dad nicknamed her "the ambulance" because when she got upset she sounded like a siren:

WAA-OOH, WAA-OOH!

As if he can read my mind, Jakey suddenly announces, "That bad baby is NOT allowed near my toys. Especially Pete."

Pete is the stuffed toy dinosaur my brother has slept with every night since he was born. My little brother has two rules:

1. Nobody is allowed to touch Pete, EVER.

2. He won't set foot in any sandbox because he's scared of being stuck in quicksand.

This morning he copied me and lined up Pete and two trucks to welcome Zara. Except he also built a barrier of books so she could look but not touch.

Jakey is being nice, but he'll never forgive Zara. When we met her for the first time, Mommy let him hold her. He was very gentle and even sang her a song . . . but then she vomited green stuff all over his new white shoes.

YUCK.

And then—would you believe it?—she laughed.

But that's not the only reason Jakey hasn't forgiven Zara. Last time she came to our house, as soon as Mommy left the room, she unscrewed the lid of her sippy cup and tipped orange juice all over Jakey's head. Then,

while he was wiping his face, Zara pulled down his shorts!

My aunt claimed it was an accident, but Jakey and I know it wasn't.

Who knows what trouble that baby will get into today now that she can crawl? At least we will have Marge to protect us.

DING DONG

Archie, our pug-nosed puppy, starts barking. I can hear Mommy's heels *click-clack* on the wooden floor as she hurries to let Zara and Aunt Sally in.

I get up from the blanket and peer through the French doors. There in the hallway is my aunt Sally with a pink baby carriage. Zara's carriage. I can feel my heart start to beat a little faster.

The back door swings open as Mommy

and Sally push the carriage outside, chatting happily. Its big wheels are chopping through the grass. I spy one of Zara's small chubby hands waving. There is no escape now.

Archie lowers his head and covers his eyes with his paws. I wish I could make a run for it, but I need to be a big girl today if I want to spend time with Marge and show her my drawings.

The carriage's wheels grind to a halt.

"What a good baby-waby you are!" gushes Sally as she scoops her daughter up.

Our little cousin does look sweet. She has curly hair, which is held back with a giant purple bow.

Jake obviously doesn't think she looks sweet, though. "With those fat thighs she could be a sumo wrestler," he whispers. Although he says this in my ear, it's like Zara has heard him.

"**Ga-ga**," she says, and points her tiny finger at me.

A shiver wriggles down my spine.

"Ga-ga?" I raise an eyebrow at Jake.

"*Ga-ga* means *I am going to get you*," Jakey whispers.

We share a nervous giggle as Zara stares

daggers at us. Hopefully Marge will know how to make her behave.

I give our aunt a big hug, careful not to squash the baby, and she tells me that I look taller. Jakey shows Sally his front tooth, which is becoming wobbly. She seems impressed.

As Sally gives Zara to Mommy, Mommy starts speaking in a baby voice.

"Hello, Zara, ba-ba boo-boo, baaa."

Why do grown-ups always talk to babies like they are stupid?

Mommy squeezes Zara's cheeks and she chuckles, acting cute.

"Marge should be here shortly," Mommy promises Sally.

They are going out for a special lunch to celebrate Sally's birthday. With Dad away working, Marge is in charge of us.

DING DONG

That's the doorbell again!

"I'll get it!" Jakey bolts past me. He's making his airplane-taking-off sound.

THUD—now he's tripped over onto the grass.

"Oww!" he shouts, annoyed. His face is redder than a fire engine.

I think he's about to say something else when Mommy reminds him, "No bad words." She gives him a hug and he jumps into his little car and rides into the house, racing for the front door.

Jakey has had a potty mouth lately. Mommy got angry when he said a bad word in front of his teacher last week, so now we have a chart on the fridge. We get one point if we use a bad word, and Jakey has three points already. If he gets five, he isn't allowed to use his bike all weekend.

The door opens and finally . . .

Marge is here!

She is wearing a plastic coat and hat and is twirling an umbrella. "I know it's not raining, but babies can be messy, so I came prepared!" Marge's smile is as big as a slice of watermelon.

Jakey scampers underneath her coat. "I hate babies!" he says, hiding.

"Me too." Marge winks as she bends down to Jakey's height, which isn't very far for her even though he is only four years old.

"Do you know who LOVES babies more than anyone?" she asks us.

"Mommy?" I guess.

Marge shakes her head.

"Who, then?" Jakey blinks.

"Pirates!" she whispers.

Our eyes widen in shock. Marge is full of surprises.

"Here," I say, holding out my drawing shyly. "I did a self-portrait."

Marge stares at it for a long time. "You are a wonderful artist, Jemima. If the queen saw this, she would frame it for all to see."

My heart is bursting with pride! I can't

wait to show Marge the rest of my drawings.

Marge is actually a duchess, which means that she is related to the royal family. It also means that she sometimes expects a horse-drawn carriage to pick us up or a butler to bring our dinner.

Just then Mommy and Aunt Sally appear to say hello. I can tell that Sally is shocked by how small Marge is. Did I tell you that our babysitter is only the size of about seven packages of cookies stacked on top of each other?

"Looking after Zara is easy breezy," my aunt brags.

Zara may be acting cute now, but Jakey and I exchange a look—we know better.

There's lots of chatter as Mommy, Marge, and Sally have a cup of tea in the kitchen and talk through the list of rules for looking after the baby. Then Mommy puts the list on the fridge.

Sally makes sure that Zara is snuggled happily asleep in Marge's arms before she whispers good-bye and tiptoes toward the front door.

"And remember," Mommy tells us quietly, "be on your best behavior and help Marge with your cousin while we're out." She kisses us both and waits for us to promise.

"I will." I smile.

But is Zara going to be on *her* best behavior?

"I won't." Jakey scowls. "The only babies I like are baby T. rexes!"

Sally and Mommy laugh, but I am a bit worried.

"If there are any bad words, put a point on the chart, please," Mommy tells Marge.

Marge nods as she gets up from the kitchen table and gently puts the baby into her carriage.

Zara's eyes are shut, but one hand is gripped in a fist. Is she really asleep?

We all traipse outside and I wave good-bye to

Mommy as she and Aunt Sally pull out down the driveway.

"Good-bye, kids, and remember—Marge is in charge!"

The minute our old blue car disappears, I turn back to the house. Jakey is playing sumo wrestlers with Marge on the grass, so I go over to check on the baby. I tiptoe very quietly, and as I peer inside the carriage I can see . . . it's empty. My palms start to sweat. I knew she was only pretending to be asleep!

I glimpse a tiny foot disappearing around the corner of the house—Zara is heading for the backyard.

"Runaway baby!" I cry, racing after her.

Marge and Jakey follow at top speed.

In the backyard, Zara has discovered Jakey's Legopirate ship.

As we sprint toward her, I notice a wicked glint in her eye. Then she lifts the ship in the air as if it's a ball she's about to throw. . . .

In one quick motion, Marge grabs her and passes me the pirate ship.

"Watch out, little scalawag," she scolds. "Or you will have to walk the plank!"

Zara gurgles in annoyance and Marge settles her back into the carriage with a pacifier.

"You see, babies are unpredictable. The only people they respect are pirates," she says.

"Pirates?" I ask. I can't picture it.

"Yes," Marge replies, sitting down on our blanket. She pulls Jakey onto her lap and I scooch in next to her.

I love it when Marge tells us a story.

"So . . . ," Marge begins as she takes off her

hat. Out pours her rainbow hair, glimmering in the sunshine.

I don't remember if I told you this, but our babysitter has red, green, yellow, orange, and blue hair! The first time I saw it I couldn't believe my eyes! I'm not sure if Mommy and Dad would let her look after us if they saw her crazy magical hair. But as it happens, she only ever takes it out when we are alone with her.

"After I left the palace, I decided to sail to Africa on my ship, the *Admiral Marge the Eighth*. I wanted to explore faraway lands and find a cure for my albino water buffalo's insomnia."

"What's insomnia?" Jake asks.

"It's the opposite of *out*somnia, which is when you sleep all the time," Marge explains. "But halfway across the ocean, my ship was attacked . . . by pirates!"

I suddenly feel nervous. Jake's bottom lip is quivering, and even Zara looks scared.

"Their ship was called the *Poison Curse* and the captain was Not-So-Jolly Roger. But he was really rather soft and sweet inside."

Captain Not-So-Jolly Roger

"He was?" Jakey gulps.

"Yes! He needed a nanny for all the babies on board. So I took the job and Wesley, my albino water buffalo, befriended the captain's parrot, Pollyanna. The only thing that pirates adore more than treasure is babies."

I don't know whether to believe Marge. I can't imagine a pirate captain cuddling a baby, no matter how soft and sweet he is!

Jake isn't sure either. "Are there really babies living at sea?" he asks.

"Hundreds of them. When you think about it," Marge reasons, "babies and pirates have a lot in common."

"They do?" we chorus.

"Of course! They both love shiny things. They take other people's stuff without asking. And they drink from bottles all day! All babies are pirates at heart."

Jakey and I turn to each other. It does make perfect sense.

"Now let's read the list of rules," Marge says, going inside to get it and coming back outside to hand it to me. "Hop to it!"

"GOOGA!" Zara cries, snatching the list from me and biting a chunk out of it.

She chews twice, then spits it out.

YUCK. It's all soggy and I can't read it now.

But Marge isn't worried. "I knew a pirate baby who chewed a whole treasure map once." Her eyes twinkle with the memory. "We don't need the list anyway. I've looked after a lot of babies at sea. We'll follow Marge's Pirate Code instead."

I don't know how my aunt will feel about this, but Marge is in charge.

Rule 1. Zara needs a bottle of milk, not rum. She's not allowed rum until she is a fully grown pirate.

Rule 2. Pirate babies need games to entertain them, treasure to play with, and lots of cuddles.

"Pirates love to snuggle babies," Marge explains. "When your job is being scary at sea all day long, there is nothing more soothing than singing sweet lullabies at night."

Jake looks at Zara and I can see his face soften. He moves over to the carriage to give her a cuddle, but my baby cousin has other ideas.

YANK! Zara grabs Jakey's hair and tugs.

"STUPID SHORT-LEGS!" Jakey hollers.

Uh-oh, that was rude of him. Mommy would not like that one bit.

Marge continues with her Pirate Code.

Rule 3. No bad words. Unless we are in battle at sea, or your parrot poops on your shoulder.

She winks at me. "Are we all on board, me hearties?"

We both nod. I can tell Jake is imagining himself in a dangerous battle at sea. Marge won't have to put a point on the chart if Jake sticks to the code.

"Then you're ready for your pirate names!"

Rule 4. Every shipmate needs a pirate name.

Jakey sticks his tongue out at Zara. "Her name can be Captain Fat Thighs!"

Zara does NOT look pleased with that name. She is beginning to look upset.

"Or Blackbeard?" suggests Marge.

It doesn't work. Zara's face is now the color of a ripe tomato.

"What about Captain Purple Bow?" I offer.

But it's too late. Zara starts to sob.

The sound of an ambulance siren begins.

WAAAAAH-OOOOOH!

Marge picks up Archie and tries a silly dance to cheer her up, but it makes no difference.

Then I remember Marge's Pirate Code—
Zara must want a bottle!

I reach for one in her diaper bag. Zara
stops crying when she sees it.

Marge pats my shoulder in relief.

Zara takes the bottle from me
and then . . .

WHEEEEEEE

with a toothy grin, she THROWS it.

We all duck our heads as the bottle flies
across the backyard, whizzes through the
open door, and rolls into our house.

Is our cousin a superbaby?

Jakey looks impressed, like the time
I accidentally exploded our homemade
volcano on Dad's work papers.

"Pirate babies love to throw things," Marge says. "Part of my job as a pirate nanny was collecting all the treasure that was tossed around the ship! The other part was only allowing babies to play with the *blunt* cutlasses. A cutlass is a sword and is very dangerous," she explains.

"WAAH-OOH!" Zara is crying again. I grab hold of the carriage handle, and we all head into the house and look for the bottle. Jakey shouts to us from in front of the sofa. Her bottle is trapped beneath it.

Jakey looks worried. "Dad says the sofa is too heavy to move. That's why he couldn't get my silver whistle."

(I bet it's not impossible to move the sofa. I know for a fact that Dad had had enough of Jakey screeching on that whistle all the time.)

We poke our heads under the sofa and Jakey tries using his tennis racket, but it doesn't reach the bottle. Although I am doing my best to blow it out like the wolf from "The Three Little Pigs," my lungs aren't strong enough.

Marge plops Zara on Dad's chair and hitches up her skirt.

"Shiver me timbers!" she says determinedly. Using the top of her umbrella, she manages to snag the bottle.

We high-five our pirate nanny and then look back at Zara.

Uh-oh. Zara is GONE!

Wasn't she on Dad's chair just a moment ago?

"Pirate babies also love to play hide-and-seek," Marge tells us. "Once I found fifteen babies hiding in a pile of cannonballs!"

Sally and Mommy will not be happy if we can't find our little cousin.

We hunt around the living room . . . no Zara.

We search Dad's office . . . no Zara.

We look in the kitchen and behind the curtains . . . no Zara.

I am starting to panic.
And what are these
puddles of water
on the floor?

There's a trail like the ones our
pet snails, Bill and Bob, leave,
but much bigger.

"She must be teething," Marge explains.
"When babies have teeth coming in, they
dribble a lot."

Eww . . .

"FOLLOW THAT DROOL!"

cries Jakey.

We follow the trail of little puddles
along the hallway. The
largest one is just
outside the coat closet.

Marge's hands are
on her hips. "The trail
ends here."

Phew, we found her!

"Gotcha!" Jakey opens the door and we discover Zara hiding among the coats, hugging my rain boot.

I wave her bottle. Is she hungry?

But she grins, scoots by us, and skedaddles down the hall.

Jakey lunges for her, and she darts between his legs.

This pirate baby is faster than a squirrel sneaking a nut. We watch in shock as my baby cousin wiggles and giggles through the living room.

Her purple bow flies behind her like a small cape.

TUG—she pulls all the magazines off the coffee table.

SMASH—she throws the TV remote across the room.

RIIIP—she tears Dad's newspaper in half.

Marge dives to tackle her, but naughty Zara sinks her teeth into Marge's outstretched finger.

"**Argh!** I shall never play the harp again!" Marge gasps in pain.

"Capture that sea robber!" Jakey orders, jumping onto the sofa and waving his tennis racket like it's a sword.

"Capture me a Band-Aid!" Marge moans, holding out her bitten finger.

Zara is now quickly crawling up the stairs. I try to grab her leg, but she squirms free, slipping around the banister and into our bedroom. I am panting as I reach the doorway.

"Don't knock over my—"

Before I can finish the sentence, disaster strikes.

The castle that I've built out of magnet tiles and filled with princess figurines has been toppled. It took me HOURS to build it! I am so mad I could scream.

Zara turns to me with a smirk.

"Ahoy, me matey!" Marge appears and snatches Zara into her arms.

Jake is now inside our room too and shaking his head in wonder.

"That pirate baby is very bad AND very fast," he says, taking in my broken castle. But he doesn't say a single bad word.

I am not having a fun time anymore. Zara is ruining our day with Marge. Not to mention the mess she's made that I will have to clean up. Jakey hates cleaning and always comes up with excuses for why he can't do it. Like the time he was "temporarily blind" from watching too much TV.

"I am going to scoot in the driveway," I huff.

I stomp downstairs with my arms crossed.

"Wait, Jemima. Please, will you feed the baby? Young buccaneers are the best at bottle duty," says Marge. She brings me Zara and the food.

Zara turns to me with big, pleading eyes.

I sulk over and sit on the sofa with my baby cousin. Zara nestles into my arms and looks up at me as she drinks from her bottle. I open the jar of applesauce too, in case she wants that after her milk.

I find myself stroking her hair. It feels soft. She is so peaceful and gentle that I am not grumpy anymore.

Just as I am thinking happy, loving thoughts, Zara tips the applesauce all over my head! It's dripping down my hair and into my eyebrows. I am covered in apple. I taste it.

"Scrumdiddleyumptious!"

I say, trying to lick my own face like a cat.

I pass Zara back to Marge and wipe my face and hair. At least now Zara is yawning and rubbing her eyes. She must need a nap. So Jakey and I help by getting a blanket and closing the curtains.

Once we have grabbed a snack from the kitchen, we take our scooters outside so Marge and Zara can have some peace and quiet.

After six races (I win two) and a cheese sandwich each, we are bored and creep back inside.

Oh no!

There, curled up asleep in the carriage, sucking on a pacifier, is MARGE!

Wide-awake and sitting cross-legged on the sofa is . . . baby ZARA.

I can't believe that our grown-up baby-sitter has fallen asleep inside a baby's carriage. It's one thing being the same height as a child, but quite another stealing their bed.

"Wake up!" Jakey pries open one of Marge's eyes.

Marge's chest is rising and falling as she snores.

I pull the pacifier out of her mouth. Marge stirs slightly but still doesn't wake up.

POP!

Now I get the giggles and Jakey keels over laughing. But it's only when Zara shrieks with delight that Marge opens a sleepy eye.

"Can I nap for another three hours?" she asks, yawning.

"No." I giggle.

"That tiny bed on wheels is so comfortable. I must get one for Wesley. It would surely cure his insomnia." Marge stretches and tries to get out of the carriage but her bottom is stuck.

We are laughing so hard our sides ache.

"Attention, pirates! Get ready to scrub the decks and let's finish the Pirate Code. Heave-ho!"

Marge's voice sounds strict, but we can't take her seriously because she's moved into a squatting position to try to wiggle free. She looks so silly.

Jakey and I salute. "Aye, aye,

Captain Marge the Sleepy!"

Even Archie joins in, sitting in a line with us. He holds up his paw to our captain, Marge the Pirate Nanny.

And for the first time that day, Zara gives us all a sparkling, happy smile, bubbling up with joy.

Finally Marge frees herself from the carriage and gives us our pirate names. We write them on name tags and stick them to our clothes.

Jakey is **Jakeypants the Fierce**.

Marge becomes **Marge the Pirate Nanny** (also known as **Marge the Sleepy**).

Archie looks surprised to be called **Salty Sea Doggy**.

Zara drools onto her new name, **Captain No Beard**.

And my pirate name is **Long John Jemima**!

The next part of Marge's Pirate Code is:

Rule 5. All shipmates must dress as pirates.

I am starting to have fun again as we get busy making our costumes. We find cotton balls, paint them, and tape them to our chins as scary hairy beards. (I color mine red to match my hair. I actually look a little like an old photograph I have seen of Dad. When he was younger, he had a fluffy red beard!)

Because I am the best at drawing, I sketch our swords and eye patches on black paper and Marge cuts them out. We even make pirate jewelry out of some old buttons from Mommy's sewing kit.

Archie looks brave with his hat but isn't happy about wearing the small black boots that I made for him.

Zara has the most terrifying costume, because Marge manages to make a hook out of a plastic coat hanger and tucks it into her onesie. She keeps waving her hook hand at us!

Then we hear a loud raspberry sound, which is followed by a foul smell in the air.

It seems to be coming from Zara.
PHEW EUK!
It stinks worse than broccoli and smelly socks.

Zara points to her diaper with her little hook hand.

"Captain No Beard did a doo-doo," Jakey complains. He is now holding his nose.

Marge looks worried. "I wish we had the Royal Nanny here to help. I've never changed a diaper before!"

"Who changed the diapers at sea?" I ask.

"Poop-Patrol Pete was in charge of Code Brown. He used his eye patch to cover his nose," Marge explains.

I have changed lots of diapers on my

dollies. And I did promise Mommy I'd help Marge today. . . . I glance at Jakey, and I know he's thinking the same as me. We both love having Marge to look after us, even if it means we have to look after her a bit sometimes, too.

"Don't worry, Captain. We will do it." I pat her shoulder reassuringly.

"Phew! Good work, me hearties." Marge the Pirate Nanny salutes us gratefully. She moves to the far side of the room, where she opens her umbrella and hides behind it. Archie's tail is between his legs.

"Ewww-eeeee!" shouts Jake as I take off the dirty diaper.

"I haven't smelled a poop this stinky since my gorilla, Edwina, overdid it with the cauliflower cheese," Marge confides from behind her umbrella.

Jakey and I make a great team. He makes faces at Zara to keep her calm (and because it smells so yucky) while I change her. We must look funny to Zara—a pair of fierce scalawag pirates changing her diaper!

"Yayaya!" Zara points her hook hand at me and Jakey when we have finished.

"That means she likes us," Jakey says.

I hope this means less biting and less dumping things on our heads in the future.

As we're washing and drying our hands, I remember how sleepy Zara was earlier. "Is there anything in the Pirate Code about bedtime for babies?"

Marge's face lights up. "Yes, I forgot!"

Rule 6. All pirates need a ship deck to sleep on and waves to rock them to sleep.

"We are going to build a ship for Zara to sleep in," Marge announces. "That will fix her insomnia."

We rush around gathering supplies, then head outside to construct a life-size pirate ship that looks as much as possible like Jakey's Lego one. Zara is happily throwing the ball for Archie. She's really good at it!

"I'll get the sail." Marge is running into the house, her magical hair fanning out behind her.

"Batten down the hatches!" I shout. Together we drag an old wooden table under the shade of the oak tree and turn it upside down. Then we put a cardboard box on top of it. We cut windows for the portholes and make an anchor out of Dad's wrench and a jump rope.

"Thar she blows!" Jakeypants the Fierce cries as he hoists Marge's "sail" onto a rake propped against the box. It looks a bit like the bedsheet from our parents' room.

"**YOOYOO!**" Zara cries, pointing to the mast and sail, which means (I hope) that she is finally ready to nap.

"All right—bedtime, little scalawag!" Marge tells her. She takes off Zara's hook and gently lays her on a blanket inside our ship.

"She needs some booty!" Jakey runs off.

He returns from the house with Pete, his stuffed dinosaur, and gives him to Zara to cuddle. I can't believe it!

Baby Zara snuggles Pete and closes her eyes, while Marge sings in her warbling cat voice.

"We love to sail the seven seas.
Yo ho, yo ho,
a pirate's life for me.
The ship's a place for sleepy babies.
Yo ho, yo ho,
a pirate's life for me."

Jakey and I tiptoe inside. I start drawing a picture of how I imagine Not-So-Jolly Roger looks. I draw his fingers and toes perfectly, and Jakey turns his Lego ship into a treasure chest.

After a while we get bored and sneak back to our ship. Captain No Beard is finally asleep. But where is Marge?

"Marge?" I whisper, peeping behind our ship.

But she doesn't reply.

Jakey checks the backyard and even inside Zara's carriage. We can't see her anywhere—our babysitter has disappeared!

Suddenly I remember that the whole house is a mess from when Zara ran away, and from us creating our wonderful pirate costumes. . . .

Just as I start worrying, we hear a car in the driveway. Uh-oh—there's no time to find Marge now, and no time to tidy up! I hope Mommy understands that we couldn't do anything on her list because Zara bit it!

"Parents AHOY!" I call in my pirate voice.

If Marge hears me, she'll know that the grown-ups are home.

As Mommy and Aunt Sally walk toward us, smiling, Marge suddenly appears on the other side of the ship, where I was just looking a moment ago. Her pirate beard is gone and all her amazing hair is hidden away under her hat. Our pirate nanny looks like a regular babysitter again.

"Hi, Jemima." Mommy gives me a hug. "You look a bit like Dad in that beard."

Sally gazes at baby Zara dozing sweetly in our pirate ship under the tree. "How was my darling baby-waby?" she asks.

"Marge was going to make Captain No Beard scrub the decks, but once we'd built her a ship, she fell asleep. Everyone gets *out*somnia at sea!" Jakey informs them.

Mommy and Sally laugh, thinking he's being silly. If only they knew.

"Is that your dinosaur Zara is holding?" Mommy asks, surprised.

Jakey shrugs as if it's no big deal. Maybe my little brother is starting to like babies.

I think I am, too. As I watch Aunt Sally gently picking up Zara and moving her back into her carriage, I wish I could give her one last cuddle myself.

I sigh as we all head inside, and then I remember the mess.

I am about to apologize, but when Mommy opens the door, the entire house is SPOTLESS!

My mouth opens and closes like a goldfish's, but no words come out. How is that possible? I look at Marge—is she magical? How did she manage to tidy up the whole house so quickly?

Marge gathers her bag and whispers to me, "As shipshape as my shipmates," as she heads to the door.

"How were the children? Did they behave themselves?" Mommy asks, looking at Jake and me expectantly.

Marge nods. "They followed the Pirate Code well! Especially Code Brown." She salutes us both farewell. "Good-bye, Long

John Jemima and Jakeypants the Fierce. Only play with the blunt cutlasses, and no bad words." Marge winks at Jakey.

"What's Code Brown?" Mommy asks when Marge has gone.

"When Captain No Beard did a doo-doo and Jakey and I changed her all by ourselves!" I say proudly.

Mommy and Sally share a glance.

We all look at my baby cousin.

"ARRRRR!" cries Zara in her sleep, just like a real pirate dreaming of a battle.

Jakey and I stare at each other in shock. Maybe babies really are pirates at heart. I guess we'll never know. . . .

Marge and the Stolen Treasure

It's a boring and very hot day. Jakeypants (my four-year-old brother) and me (Jemima Button) are both in the backyard. He's playing in a big cardboard box, and I can tell he's getting tired and sticky. I'm reading my book in the shade. Not a single branch or leaf on any of the trees is moving. There are no clouds in the sky. And despite reading my book in the shade, I am sweatier than a polar bear on the beach.

DING DONG

Jakey and I look at each other. We aren't expecting any visitors today, are we?

"It's your babysitter, Marge," Mommy calls as she heads to the front door. "She's going to take you to the pool to meet your cousin Zara for a swim."

Wait. We have to spend the day with Zara?? Mommy never told us that. She knows, with Marge coming, we'll still agree to go. But we aren't happy about it.

YAY for Marge! I can't do a somersault or snap my fingers yet, but I am a really good swimmer. Mommy thinks that I could be part dolphin because I can hold my breath underwater for so long. But wouldn't I be gray or have a fin? Jakey refuses to put his face underwater. EVEN A LITTLE.

We race inside. I am so excited. Marge is not a regular babysitter. She grew up in a palace with lots of amazing pets and doesn't act like a grown-up at all!

"MARGE!" we shout gleefully. She is standing in the doorway, no taller than a Christmas elf. Her hair is hidden under a bathing cap and she is wearing a pink robe and gold sandals.

"Lords, ladies, gentlemen . . . and animal friends," she announces in a fancy voice. Archie, our pug-nosed puppy, has appeared and yaps back at her. "Prepare to swim with Margery Beauregard Victoria Ponterfois!"

She whips a pink fan out of her bag and cools her face.

"Thanks for coming at such short notice, Marge," Mommy says gratefully, and she heads back into the kitchen looking for something.

"My wombats are competing in the Marsupial Olympics, and Camilla Camel is getting a much-needed facial," reveals Marge. "So I had the afternoon free as it turns out." She slides the fan, along with a sparkly key ring, back into her bag.

I can hear Mommy and Dad walking all over the house looking for their car keys. They have to go to the supermarket.

Dad's face is red. "Jakey, have you hidden the car keys again?" he asks, sounding angry.

My little brother pretends not to hear. His new favorite game is hiding things. Yesterday he hid my crayons behind the radiator, and last week I was searching for my best purple socks for EONS before Jakey confessed that he had buried them in the backyard. Mommy was furious when she dug them up, because they had a worm in them, and I had to wear my sandals even though it was raining.

"JAKEY!!"

Finally he admits the keys are in the laundry basket. "I am the best hider ever," he whispers to Marge.

"No, Princess Chantelle was the best hider ever. She hid King Eugene's false teeth and they were never found," Marge whispers back. "He could only eat Jell-O and custard after that."

Yum! I wouldn't mind that.

Mommy reminds Marge that her list is on the fridge and that we have to behave nicely.

As we hug our parents good-bye, I act like I will miss them, but secretly I won't. Having Marge around is the best fun in the world.

As the door shuts, Marge peels off her bathing cap and out flows her incredible rainbow hair. Then she whips off her robe, and underneath she is wearing a polka-dot swimsuit!

"Get the list," Marge orders, doing a high kick. "Hop to it!"

Jakey mimes diving into a pool and then pretends to swim all the way to the kitchen. When he brings the list back, I read it aloud while Marge fans Archie, who is panting.

1. No swimming without sunscreen or a hat.

2. There are sandwiches and carrots for lunch.

3. The pool is a 10-minute walk away, and clean towels are in the laundry basket.

Jakey hates carrots, so he takes the list from me and folds it in half, then into quarters. He keeps on folding until it's the size of a marble before eventually hiding it inside a matchbox. Mommy will not like that one little bit.

Marge flops into Dad's chair and wipes her forehead.

"I haven't been this hot since I galloped across the Arabian Desert on my black stallion, Sebastian Seranado." She sighs dreamily. "He was my first love. . . ."

My beloved, Sebastian ♥

"Why were you in the Arabian Desert?" I ask.

"I was on a royal expedition, of course."

"What is an expedition?"

"Explorers go on expeditions to Find Things Out. To peer into unknown corners of the world and discover new animals."

Jakey jumps up and down. "Can we go on an expedition to the pool?"

Marge nods enthusiastically. "Jemima, you are head of the planning committee."

I run for my silver notebook and the ballpoint pen with a feather on top.

"What do explorers need to take with them?" My pen is poised.

"We will need . . . ," Marge begins.

"A map?" Jakey pipes up. Even though Jakey and I know the way to the pool, Marge doesn't.

Marge nods her head and I write it in my Explorer's Notebook. "A map can also help explorers mark down new places and creatures that they discover on their travels."

Jakey finds a giant sheet of yellow construction paper and we draw our road, Wells Street. Marge sticks a gold star in the middle and labels it Jake & Jemima's place. I draw a house nearby and mark it Lucy, Theo, and Matthew's house. Last of all, Jakey pours green glitter on a dab of glue at the bottom and writes Pool.

"Right. The next thing we need is some Marge's Marvelous Explorers Lemonade," Marge says, smacking her lips.

I don't know if Mommy will be happy when she sees that Marge has emptied all the tulips from the big blue china vase—our babysitter is now filling it with ice cubes and water to use as a jug!

We should be careful with the vase. Sometimes Jakey accidentally smashes things. Like when he used Dad's special red mug to smuggle dirt in from the backyard. But I am having too much fun making the lemoniest lemonade to worry. We squeeze in lots of lemon juice and then it's ready.

"Let's taste it!" Marge pours us tall glasses and we clink them together. After a few sips she insists that we all link arms and sip from each other's glasses. But we get in a terrible tangle! My arm is somehow twisted around Marge's back, and Jakey's leg is over my shoulders, and soon we look like a human octopus in a knot and our lemonade is spilling everywhere!

Marge glugs Jakey's lemonade . . . SLURP!

Jakey guzzles mine. FANTASTICO!

I gulp from Marge's glass. YUM!

Archie laps his up. LICK!

* * *

Packing for the expedition takes a little while. I can't find my swimsuit at first. It turns out Jakey has dressed Pete the dinosaur in it and then hidden him in the hallway closet. Then Marge mistakes Archie's dog blankets for the pool towels and packs Dad's shaving cream instead of the sunscreen.

I roll up our map and put our lunch into Jakey's backpack. Around his neck Jakey is wearing our binoculars—we made them out of toilet paper rolls so we could spy on our parents during their dinner parties. (By the way, it turns out that nothing fun happens at dinner parties. They're not parties AT ALL. Grown-ups just sit, talk, and eat.)

As we leave the house, I grab our butterfly net, and we're off!

Marge has balanced the big china vase of

lemonade on Jake's red wagon. Jakey agrees
he will pull it along the street . . . but he is
not so agreeable on the subject of sunscreen.

"It was on Mommy's list. You have to wear it!" I tell him.

Now, my little brother has two rules (in addition to no sandboxes and no sharing his dinosaur):

1. He will never eat crusts. Even on pizza.

2. He refuses to wear sunscreen.

Jakey looks determined as he shakes his head. "NO sunscreen. Ever."

I am feeling upset now since I really wanted to go swimming, and everything else is ready. I am not crying but my eyes are starting to feel tickly.

Marge sees my face and thinks for a moment.

"All explorers need to be

protected from wild animals. Did you know that sunscreen scares tigers and lions away?"

Jakey looks surprised.

Marge continues. "Jumping spiders are allergic to sunscreen, too."

Jakey's eyes grow wider.

"And it's also been known to stop ladies from falling in love with you!"

"I want sunscreen!" Jakey cries, slathering it all over his face and arms.

WHOOPEE!

At last we set off down the street. I am at the front, reading the map to help us find our way. Next comes Jakey, pulling along the red wagon with the huge vase wobbling on top. Archie trots behind us, his little paws moving quickly like he's a baby ballerina. At the back is Marge. She is using the binoculars to look for zebras and exotic plants and singing in her warbling voice:

"Explorers come from near and far,

Come by foot or come by car.

Today we venture to the pool.

Let us be brave and keep our cool!"

During our walk we find an ant column snaking along the sidewalk and into the long grass. Crouching down and using the binoculars, we manage to spot the ants marching through the blades of grass and up onto a tiny hill. There we discover the hole that leads to their underground world!

I peer inside. I would love to shrink down to the size of an ant, just for one day, to see what it's like.

"An explorer has to record what they discover," instructs Marge.

So Jakey draws a picture on the map and I label it ANT CITY. Then I take my Explorer's Notebook out and sketch an ant wearing a top hat!

It is really hot and sunny, and the red wagon is quite slow on the lumpy sidewalk.

So we flop down outside Theo's house. Theo is Jakey's best friend and I am friends with Lucy, his big sister, but she is away at camp. Theo and his little brother, Matthew, run out to greet us.

"Where are you going?" they ask, eyeing our marvelous supplies.

"We are on an expedition to the pool!" Jakey explains in an important voice.

Theo is peering into the vase. "Is that lemonade?"

Marge pours us each a drink. "Explorers always share whatever they have on an expedition. When I was in Thailand, I came across an orangutan named Oscar with terribly tangled fur. I shared the last of my conditioner with him. After a good scrub we combed out every single knot!"

Marge's face is so serious

when she tells us this that Matthew and I get the giggles.

When the lemonade is finished, it's time to be on our way. We wave good-bye to our friends and agree to meet them later at the pool.

The wagon is lighter now and easier to drag, until Archie, who is too hot to walk, jumps into it and we have to pull him along as well. He curls up around the cool vase, napping.

We trundle on down the street. Marge is making bird calls with her hands, but to be honest she sounds more like an angry chicken squawking.

"At the palace we had an official Bird Whisperer called Augustus. Augustus could talk to any feathered friend, and he once saved four and twenty blackbirds from being baked in a pie. He taught me lots of bird calls." She quacks loudly, like a duck. Then she gobbles like a turkey. Jakey snorts with laughter.

The birds in the trees lining the street are curious and circle us, chirping. I've never seen birds behave like this before. I am watching carefully so that I can write it all in my Explorer's Notebook later. Then Jakey joins in by howling like a wolf and they fly away!

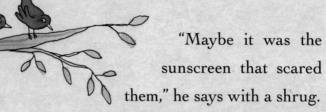

"Maybe it was the sunscreen that scared them," he says with a shrug.

The others haven't noticed, but I have spotted a bird's nest in the oak tree beside us. As I watch it, a tiny yellow beak pokes out. It's a baby bird.

"Look!"

They look where I am pointing and spot it too. Marge clucks to the bird for a long time.

"What are you doing, Marge?" I ask.

"It's a prayer that the chick will learn to fly soon. That's what Augustus would do if he were here."

I mark a tiny love heart on the map where I saw the nest. I can't believe how lucky I am to have glimpsed a baby chick! I really am an explorer now.

The pavement leads us down to the main

road. We're nearly at the swimming pool! Before crossing the street, Marge makes us wait, holding hands, looking left and right.

"Sunscreen doesn't protect against speeding cars," she says seriously.

We can hear shrieking and squeals of laughter as we arrive at the entrance. The pool is shaped like a letter *L*, and there is an ice-cream shop and some shady trees to sit under. The deep end has a diving board, and Lifeguard Steve sits next to it. He is short and round and shaped like a doughnut. Jakey calls him Shouty Steve because he always shouts instead of using his whistle. He didn't even blow his whistle a few weeks ago when Theo ate an ice cream *in* the pool. He shouted so loudly that day, I could hear him underwater.

Once we've parked our wagon and spread

out the blanket under a big tree, we change into our swimsuits. Then we hear a familiar voice. . . .

"Goo-gaaah!"

I whip my head around. Our little cousin Zara (the naughtiest baby ever) is racing toward us in her swim diaper. She is wearing floaties, a blue blow-up ring around her middle, and flippers on her tiny feet. Aunt Sally looks pooped, huffing and puffing behind her in a sun hat.

Zara only recently learned to walk, so everyone thinks it's an "accident" when she steps on our toes, but Jakey and I know differently.

"You're all here at last! Can you take my sweet angel for a dip while I change into my swimsuit?" asks our aunt.

She's got that wrong. Zara is no angel—she

is a pirate baby who likes to make mischief.

"Of course," Marge replies.

"I'll be back in five minutes!"

Sitting on the edge of the pool, we dangle our legs in the cool water. It feels wonderful on such a hot day.

Until suddenly I feel a pair of little hands on my back!

Zara just pushed me in! I have water in my eyes and up my nose.

Jakey lands beside me in the water next.

Then Marge is suddenly splashing next

to us!

SPLOOSH

Zara is smiling wickedly when we pop up, spluttering and bedraggled.

Marge swims over to the side and gives Zara's floaties a pinch. "Explorers should always be prepared to expect surprises."

Marge has pulled Zara into the pool, too!

SPLOSH

Our little cousin is laughing as she bobs on the surface, splashing us.

Now Zara thinks this game is hilarious and wants to be pulled in again and again. Each time, she kicks her legs and tries to make a bigger and bigger splash. It's fun at first, but after about twenty times it gets a little boring.

"Did you know that I am on the Royal Synchronized Swimming Team?" Marge reveals, doing a showy flip.

I hold Zara in my arms while Marge floats on her back and shows us her moves. She crosses and recrosses her legs in the air while twirling underwater. She looks quite majestic in her polka-dot swimsuit, like a spotted sea lion performing tricks. Then my aunt shows up and takes Zara back. At last, I'm free to swim in the deep end!

"Bye, Zara!" Marge and Jakey and I wave cheerfully.

I swim over and see my friends Emily and Sarah jumping off the diving board. I wish I had the courage to do that, but I am scared of doing a belly flop in front of everyone.

Marge suggests that we play Explorers Looking for Treasure. The game means swimming along the bottom of the pool to find coins and anything else people have dropped in the water by mistake. But Jakey is too scared. He hates getting his face wet.

"Real explorers go underwater," I explain.

"Explorers often do things they don't feel comfortable with," agrees Marge. "That's what makes them brave."

Suddenly she has an idea. We watch as she darts over to her bag and comes back

 carrying a pair of strange-looking, very old goggles.

"These are my flying goggles," she tells us, stroking them wistfully. "When I flew over the Atlantic Ocean in my twin-jet plane, *Aviatrix Marge the Fourth*, I used these goggles to keep the bugs from getting stuck in my eyelashes. All pilots need goggles— and sometimes explorers need them, too."

Jakey and I are gobsmacked. Marge is the most amazing adventurer!

I help adjust the goggles to fit Jakey's head and, would you believe it, he ducks underwater and starts to swim!

I am so proud of him. I can't wait to tell Mommy and Dad.

I show Marge my attempt at synchronized swimming, which is less majestic sea lion and more wriggly squid, while Jake uses the goggles to look for fish. Then together we search for treasure at the bottom of the pool.

Jakey and I find two coins, a single pearl earring, and a hair clip with an orange plastic flower on the side. We bring our pretty trinkets up to the surface, making a little pile on the side of the pool to take home.

When I come up for air again, I look over at Emily, who is now on the diving board doing a beautiful swan dive. I wish I could swan dive from the diving board. Or even do a regular dive from there. I've practiced lots of times from the edge of the pool.

Marge is watching me.

"Do you want to go on the diving board?" she asks, but I shake my head.

"What are you afraid of?

You are my bravest explorer!"

"Everyone will stare at me," I stammer. "I don't know if I can do it."

Her eyes light up and she swims over to me. "I have a plan."

Marge is going to create a diversion. A diversion means that she will make lots of noise at one end of the pool so everyone will look toward her. At that exact time, I will try a dive from the diving board—without anyone watching me. My heart is thumping like crazy just imagining our plan in action.

Jakey is happy because Theo and Matthew have arrived. Matthew is scraping our butterfly net along the bottom of the pool to recover even more treasure.

Marge and I have worked out a special signal. When I tap my nose twice, she will begin the diversion. My palms are sweaty as I jog across the scorching tiles to the big silver diving board, passing Emily and Sarah on the way.

As I climb up the steps, I feel as nervous as I did before the spelling bee. It's not *too* high and the water looks blue and inviting, but everyone is staring at me. I inhale deeply, then look over to Marge and tap my nose twice. It's time for her diversion.

She gives me the thumbs-up. Then she makes a very loud oinking-pig sound and starts thundering toward the water, shouting.

CAAAANNNOOONNBBBAAAALLLL!

Marge leaps off the side of the pool, crunches her body up, and hurls herself like a cannonball. She soars through the air and into the water, creating a massive splash. I hope Zara is watching.

Quickly I grit my teeth in determination as I put both my hands into a clap position, tuck my chin to my chest, and dive neatly into the water.

SPLASH!

It feels so soothing in the cool pool, and I pop my head up proudly. I can't believe it, but I did a dive from the board! All by myself. No one has noticed. They are all still shocked and spluttering from the tidal wave created by Marge's massive cannonball.

Lifeguard Steve is totally drenched and his face is turning from pink to flaming red.

For the first time ever, he blows his whistle. He must be really angry. His cheeks are purple and bulging like a giant hamster's.

Steve points to Marge and shouts, **"YOU, KIDDO, OUT OF THE POOL!"**

WHHHEEEEEP!

Marge looks at me and taps her nose proudly as she pulls herself out of the water. Her bottom has eaten her swimsuit, so everyone laughs as she heads over to Lifeguard Steve for a scolding. I can see Jakey getting out of the pool too and standing up for Marge. I think he's also explaining that she isn't really a child but our small royal babysitter.

I am so astonished by my own bravery that I quickly clamber up to try another dive, making my body even more streamlined by tucking my elbows in. I don't mind that everyone can see me now as I do another swan dive into the water.

SWOOSH!

I spend the rest of the morning trying different dives from the board. I can do a pencil dive, a starfish dive, and a duck dive. Marge watches, giving me scores out of ten for each one until it's lunchtime.

"Ice cream first!" she cries, finding her wallet. "An ice cream will help us get an appetite for lunch."

I giggle. Mommy always says it's the other way round—that we need to eat lunch before we have a sweet treat—but Marge is in charge!

I choose a strawberry Popsicle and Jakey and Marge get mint chocolate chip ice-cream cones while Archie has to settle for a bowl of water. We flump back onto our blanket, next to my aunt and baby Zara. Sally tells us that Zara isn't allowed ice cream yet. Zara is not pleased.

"GAAAA," she growls, pointing at my Popsicle.

"No, not for you, my darling baby-waby. Have this!" my aunt pleads. She is trying to spoon applesauce into Zara's closed mouth.

Suddenly Zara knocks the spoon so that applesauce splashes on everyone. Aunt Sally is starting to look mad. As quick as her nimble little legs can carry her, Zara slips out of her mom's arms and crawls over to Jakey. She grabs his ice cream and makes a dash for it. As she hurries away, she whips off her swim diaper and throws it defiantly into the air.

I chase after Zara, Jakey chases after me, and Marge is right behind us. I think Aunt Sally is still in shock on the blanket.

"NO RUNNING, KIDDOS!" shouts Steve.

We are finally able to corner our cousin near the entrance. We are all out of breath. The ice cream is melting down Zara's arm and she is wearing a naughty expression.

"Freeze, pirate baby!" I cry sternly.

"Give me back my ice cream," Jake begs.

Zara shakes her head.

Marge talks to us in a calm voice.

"Explorers often meet different types of people who don't speak the same language. We have to find another way to communicate."

I can see that Jakey would like to communicate by wrestling Zara, so I jump in quickly and try sign language (which I am learning at school), but Zara ignores me.

We both try miming. Jakey pretends to be Zara and I pretend to be him, but Zara just looks bored.

Then I have the brilliant idea of swapping Marge's flying goggles for the ice cream.

Marge approves. "Pirate babies love trinkets."

Zara hands over the ice cream and puts Marge's goggles on. She looks like a big-eyed frog, but at least she's happy. At last we all trudge back to the blanket. I'm pooped.

"Explorers often climb high trees so they can escape from wild animals and watch their enemies from afar," Marge whispers to us.

"Good idea," says Jakey. "Zara is definitely a wild animal."

First, though, Jakey and I need to hide our treasure. I lift up our blanket and dig a little hole in the ground. Then we wrap the coins and other bits up in our sandwich wrappers, bury the precious package, and put the blanket back on top.

"X marks the spot," says Marge, so I take out our map and mark the hiding place with a giant X.

Luckily the tree we're sitting under has a wide base and long branches that are easy to swing onto. This is about as perfect a climbing tree as you could ever find. The middle branch is so wide that we can sit

side by side on it. The leaves are like tiny
umbrellas shading us from the sun. It's cool
and dark up here.

Marge swings back down and up again,
getting our lunch.

Jake looks suspiciously at the carrots until Marge reminds him that explorers can't be picky eaters, and then he gobbles everything up. Mommy will be so pleased.

From my high vantage point in the tree I can see Lifeguard Steve climbing down from his chair.

"Someone has stolen my whistle," he shouts angrily. "Whoever has taken it, please give it back!"

I see the tops of everyone's heads bobbing and weaving as they start searching everywhere. I wonder to myself if Jakey has hidden it, and I am about to ask him when I spot Mommy and Dad over by the entrance.

Whoopee!

I never realize how much I have missed my mommy until I see her again. Aunt

Sally and Zara are making their way over to greet them.

We race down the tree as fast as we can, and together with Archie we run over for a hug.

Mommy goes to kiss Jakey but he pushes her away.

"I've got sunscreen on, Mommy, so you can't fall in love with me today." She laughs. "I can swim underwater now, too!" he brags. "But only with Marge's flying goggles."

"How was your swim, Jemima dolphin?" Mommy gives me a hug.

"Guess what!" I say shyly. "I dived off the diving board. All by myself."

Mommy and Dad cheer loudly and Dad ruffles my hair. "Well done, Jem."

"The children are truly fearless explorers," Marge adds, looking proud and sensible with her rainbow hair hidden under her swim cap. Is this really the same person who cannonballed into the pool oinking like a pig an hour ago?

Our parents explain that it's time to go home now, so we need to get our things. Sally and Zara are going to walk with us.

"I want to show you our treasure first," Jakey says.

"We found it at the bottom of the pool." I unroll our map to show them the X. "This is where it's secretly buried."

We head off back to our camp under the shady tree to dig it up. But when we lift the blanket, the hole is empty. All our treasure is gone! Jakey and I stare at each other open-mouthed. Someone has taken our loot. But who? Nobody knew it was there. I look at Marge, who is just as shocked as we are.

Dad says we don't have time to search for

it but promises we can find more treasure the next time we come swimming.

So we all walk home together with Aunt Sally and Zara. Jakey and I tell our parents about having a picnic in a tree and I show Mommy the drawings in my Explorer's Notebook. She really likes the one of the ant wearing a top hat. No one even asks why we are dragging a big blue china vase behind us on a wagon! Mommy is probably just relieved that Jakey didn't accidentally smash it.

When we get back to our house, it's time for Marge to head home, too. She gives us a big hug as she rummages inside her handbag and brings out her sparkly key chain.

But her car keys are no longer on it!

"Jakey, have you hidden Marge's keys?" Dad's eyebrows are raised, but my little brother shakes his head.

Slowly it dawns on me—I know who stole Marge's keys! I glance at Jakey and we both turn toward the one person we know who would steal treasure . . . **Zara the pirate baby.**

Zara giggles, and we notice that behind her back she is hiding her swim diaper. I can see that Mommy suspects her, too.

"Please can I have that?"

Mommy tries to pry the diaper from Zara's grip and she resists. A tense tug-of-war follows, which Mommy finally wins.

She opens the diaper.

Marge, Mommy, Dad, Sally, Jakey, and I all GASP!

Inside is ALL our treasure, including the orange plastic flower hair clip, but also Marge's keys along with her magical flying goggles and, last but not least, Lifeguard Steve's whistle!

"You can take the baby off the pirate ship, but you can't stop her from hunting for treasure!" Marge chuckles, shaking her head.

The grown-ups look a bit confused, but I couldn't agree more.

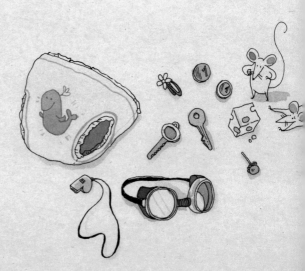

Marge and the Wacky Wedding

I wish you could see me right now. It's me, Jemima Button, and I am wearing a fancy yellow dress.

CLICK CLACK

My shoes have a tiny heel and make a tapping sound when I walk. I have a crown made of actual daisies, too. Guess why! I am being a flower girl today! I can't wait. I have never been to a wedding before, except when I made my Barbie doll marry Jakey's dinosaur.

Jakeypants is wearing a yellow suit and tie. "I look like a banana," he says, annoyed.

We are sitting on the front steps waiting

for our babysitter, Marge. Dad is gone, helping set up for the wedding this morning, and Mommy has lots of jobs to do, so Marge is coming to take care of us.

Our uncle Desmond is marrying his fiancée, Annie. Annie has pointy teeth, so Jakey has nicknamed her Annie Alligator. She babysat us once when Jakey was two and I was five, and my naughty little brother deliberately locked her in the bathroom and hid the key inside his shoe! I like Annie, but she hasn't babysat for us since. Which isn't a bad thing, I suppose, because now Marge is our babysitter and she is the most fun grown-up in the world.

For the wedding today, did I tell you that I have a wicker basket? It's filled with white rose petals that smell like summer. We are supposed to toss them on the bride and groom after the vows, so Jakey and I are practicing on our puppy, Archie.

"Walkies," I call, and he trots toward us. We have handfuls of petals hidden behind our backs.

"NOW!" Jakey shouts, and we dump the petal confetti on Archie's head.

He keeps barking playfully at us and trotting away, but he always comes back when I call him. After a while we have to stop because we are running out of petals. My little brother loves chucking confetti.

I hope he doesn't get too excited and throw the whole basket at Annie's head.

"My tie is itchy!" Jakey says angrily as he stomps off to complain to Mommy. I yawn and peer out the window, looking up and down the street again, but there's no sign of Marge.

Then I spot a blurry red shape in the distance. It's a scooter, zigzagging speedily down the street with a small person perched on the back.

That absolutely, most definitely, has to be Marge.

I run and find Jakey, who is burying his tie in the kitchen trash can.

DING DONG

We race to the door. I can't wait for Marge to see us all dressed up.

WOW! Marge looks really put together and sleek today—apart from the glittery purple motorbike helmet on her head. She flips up the visor.

"Sorry I'm late. I was painting a portrait of Natasha, my potbellied pig." She gives us both a warm hug. Marge smells like a blown-out candle—it must be her scooter. "You both look very dapper, as if you are off to a royal ball."

"TIES ARE STUPID," Jakey's voice booms. He is the loudest child in our school. I can often hear him from my classroom, which is all the way at the other end of the building.

Marge takes off her helmet and pops it onto Jakey's head. It's almost bigger than his body! "Now no one will know it's you," she tells him.

"And no one will hear you, either," I tease him, sliding down the visor.

We both turn to stare at Marge. Her long rainbow hair is sculpted into a wave. She

looks like a colorful cockatoo.

"Hi, Marge," Mommy calls, heading for Jakey. She has rescued his tie from the trash. Mommy is the maid of honor, which is a very busy and serious job. She seems a bit stressed as she wrestles Jakey's tie back on.

"The list is on the fridge," says Mommy, finally catching sight of our babysitter. "What an unusual rainbow hat, Marge!"

Jakey and I share a look. We know that Marge isn't wearing a hat.

Marge smiles and does a little curtsy. "I wore it when I was bridesmaid number twenty-nine for the Duchess of Winkerstink."

Mommy laughs, and I can tell that she thinks Marge is joking about her royal connections. But Jakey and I know better.

"Well, thank you so much for coming,

Marge. It's good to have such a responsible, reliable babysitter. Especially today."

Jakey looks at me and rolls his eyes.

If there is one thing Marge is not, it's responsible. I once had to talk her out of building a tower with all our furniture.

When Mommy heads back upstairs to take the big fat sausage curlers out of her hair, Marge describes how the Duchess of Winkerstink wanted to arrive at her wedding in a gold hot-air balloon. But after a breakfast of baked beans, she suffered a terrible bout of gas. Apparently her windy bottom pushed

THE DUCHESS OF WINKERSTINK
a wedding gone with the wind

the balloon in the wrong direction and she crash-landed in Spain instead.

"Let's see Mommy's list," Marge says, clapping her hands together. "Hop to it!"

We mount our imaginary horses and gallop into the kitchen. My horse is a little slower, so Jakey beats me and grabs the list.

Jakey is learning to read. Even though he says that he hates books, he actually read four pages of a chapter book to Mommy yesterday.

"C'mon, Jakey, you can read the first line and I will read the rest," I encourage him.

My little brother drops the paper to the floor and crosses his arms. "NO!" This is clearly not one of his reading days.

"What are you doing up there?" asks Marge. She has retrieved the list and is now crawling underneath the kitchen table. "Indeed, no one can read a list unless they are inside the Reading Cave. C'mon!"

I lift up our tablecloth and peek at her. She is all scrunched up in a little ball and wearing a goofy smile.

"Do Reading Caves have bears?" asks Jakey.

"No. Bears prefer to eat books—not read them. Hurry up. There's only room for two more!" She pats the space next to her.

My brother ducks down and bunny-hops over to Marge. I crawl in behind him, thinking how clever our babysitter can be.

We move the chairs to close up the cave and sit beside Marge. She peers at the list and pulls her silver pen out of her bag.

"Help me with this part, Jakey?"

And the next thing I know, my little brother has read three lines.

1. Please entertain the kids (and keep them quiet) in the back room until the ceremony begins.

Marge opens her purse, and inside there are paints and crayons, beads and glitter. It looks as if she's packed a whole art cupboard.

"Every artist needs supplies," she tells us. "Today we shall paint the bride and groom in all their glory."

Next to the first rule she writes: Paint all day.

I am so excited! I love painting, and art

is my favorite subject at school. We read on:

2. Jemima and Jakey will walk down the aisle before the bride and groom.

Now it's Marge who looks excited. "All eyes will be on you, so be sure to smile as big as the moon and do jazz hands."
We grin and keep reading.

3. Jemima will carry the rings on a little pillow and present them to the bride when the justice of the peace calls up the ring bearer.

"The ring bearer is the most important job at the wedding," I explain. "The rings are made of gold and must not be lost."
Jakey nods seriously and Marge agrees. I am quite proud of having been given such a big responsibility.

4. Do not let the kids near the cake or
the chocolate fountain.

Marge scribbles furiously. Now it reads,
Let the kids swim in the chocolate fountain.

We both start to laugh as Marge mimes
doing the backstroke. Then Jakey "swims"
off toward the bathroom.

Marge winks at me. "Let's finish the list."

5. When the service is over, please
encourage the kids to throw their
petals gently at the bride and groom.

Marge scribbles next to it and I read:
Throw real roses, not just petals. It
will be more dramatic!

"I don't know if that is a good idea," I say.
"Thorns are sharp." Marge looks disap-
pointed, but she crosses it out and moves on.

6. Please help Jakey use a quiet voice during the service.

We hear a flushing sound and he appears in the doorway.

"Did you wash your hands?" I ask.

"I won't!" Jakey insists, crawling back to us grumpily.

My brother has two rules:

1. He won't leave the house without his plastic sword.

2. He hates washing his hands. He says that it's boring and that germs were invented by grown-ups to stop him from having fun.

Suddenly we hear Mommy dashing past. "Where are the flower bouquets?" She sounds worried. "They should be here by now." She looks out the window. "We can't wait much longer or we'll be late."

"Don't worry, leave it to us," Marge says. "Ready, my little *florists*?"

So Jakeypants, Marge, and I run around our garden collecting wildflowers. We find bluebells, daffodils, violets, poppies, and lavender. Mommy sorts them into bunches, and we tie them together with white ribbons. Some of Jakey's flowers still have soil-covered roots, but Mommy is thrilled.

"Let's go!"

Mommy revs the engine as we all pile into our old blue car. My little brother has sneaked his plastic sword under his arm. I hope he doesn't do anything to spoil the wedding. Jakey doesn't really understand weddings. He says that he loves Mommy and is going to marry her when he grows up. I am sure Dad will have something to say about that.

Mommy leads us in a sing-along as we drive down our road and swerve around the corners and past the park, the grocery store, and the bakery until at last we're at the town hall. This is it.

Inside, the hall is beautifully decorated with white roses and lilies. Mommy says they are Annie's favorites. Everywhere smells of flowers! There is a beautiful chandelier with lots of triangles of glass twinkling in the light.

My palms are starting to feel sweaty. Today is a big day for me. Everyone is going to see me walk down the aisle and present the rings to the bride and groom. I hope I don't drop them!

"I have to show the guests to their seats," Mommy explains as people start to arrive. She points us to a back room where we can hide out until the wedding begins. That way, no one will see our special outfits until we walk down the aisle.

Marge flings open the door and we run around exploring.

"This will be our artists' studio!"

The room is empty except for a table holding a large glass bowl filled with mints. Jakey shovels some into his basket before Marge moves it away. I hide the ring pillow on the windowsill, where the rings will be safe.

WOOF WOOF

I catch Jakey's eye. I know that bark. We turn to see where the sound has come from.... There's something wriggling under Marge's coat. Out pops Archie!

Oh no! Dogs are not invited to weddings.

Marge doesn't seem surprised. "An artist needs a muse," she says. "He can be ours."

Archie's tail wags happily as he covers my face in licks.

"What's a muse?" Jakey asks.

"A muse inspires artists. What shall we paint, Archie?" Marge asks our puppy.

I don't know if I told you this, but our babysitter can communicate with animals. She once helped a 130-year-old sea turtle make friends with a blind dolphin. Apparently the turtle would ride on the dolphin's back and shout, "Go left," or "Go right," and they stayed together for ten years until one day the turtle fell off.

Archie yaps twice.

"Exactly!" Marge nods to Archie before explaining that our puppy wants us to decorate Annie and Desmond's car so that the bride and groom can leave in style. I am impressed that Marge got all that from two yaps.

As soon as all the art supplies are out, we begin making streamers and love-heart paper chains as decorations. I can't wait to see our uncle's and Annie's faces when they see their special, crazy car.

Then Theo and his little brother, Matthew, arrive with Aunt Sally and baby Zara.

Uh-oh. A wedding is an important event, and I doubt Zara understands that. She better not ruin Annie's special day. I am now glad that Jakey brought his plastic sword.

"I don't think Zara will stay quiet during the vows. Can I leave her with you?" Sally asks Marge, plopping Zara in her arms.

Mommy told me that the vows are the part where the bride and groom promise to be together forever.

Zara is dressed up like an angel with a giant pink bow on her head. She tries to pull it off, but her mommy warns her, "No bow, no go." Then Aunt Sally pecks her daughter on the head, calls good-bye to "sweet baby-waby," and leaves.

Jakey and I glance at each other. We both know that our cousin isn't a sweet angel. We suspect she is actually a pirate baby! When her parents go to sleep at night, Zara probably ransacks the house and makes her toys walk the plank. She certainly knows how to make a mess.

"Ga-ga!" she cries, pointing at Marge and grinning, her one sharp tooth glinting like a dagger.

Jake is happily painting blue stars, but I am feeling a little bit nervous. Zara is definitely the kind of baby who could ruin a wedding. Mommy told me that getting married is one of the most special days in a grown-up's life. I look at Theo and Matthew, who are fighting over the stapler. Zara is trying to reach for the scissors, and Jakey and Archie are playing fetch with a glue stick. How is Marge going to stay in charge of us all today?

She seems to read my thoughts and smiles. "You can't be worse than bonobo chimps,

Jemima. And I took five of those to tea at the Dorchester Hotel once. Chimps are just like children. They also like to fling their own poop."

But she has spoken too soon, as at that moment Zara paints a black mustache on my pink love heart! I feel my eyes tickle with tears. I know she did it on purpose.

I run to the bathroom and try to wipe the paint off with toilet paper, but it doesn't work.

Marge appears, holding a bottle from her bag. "Try Marge's magic paint potion," she suggests. "I never leave home without it."

We squirt it onto Marge's paintbrush— **SPLODGE!** It is bright green and sticky.

Is this really going to help? I wonder.

Marge sees my face and winks.

Slowly I dab at my painting with the

brush of green goo . . . and the yucky black mustache washes away! My love-heart is still there underneath, looking perfect.

PHEW!

Back in the main room, Zara is pulling the tops off felt-tip pens and throwing them at the boys.

"When does the wedding start?" I ask.

Marge runs to the window. "Now! The bride is arriving. Hide the decorations!"

We all put our art away and I wash my hands just in time. Annie has appeared at the door. I gasp. She looks like a human marshmallow, but also beautiful. Jakey is so excited that he runs over and gives her a giant hug.

Annie smiles. "Hello, Jake. I just came to use the bathroom. I'm a bit nervous."

Marge nods and points her toward it.

Oh no.

Jakey didn't wash his hands. He has left two bright blue handprints on the back of Annie's dress!

Annie has to walk down the aisle in a minute. Luckily she hasn't noticed . . . yet. Marge's mouth is wide open in a perfect O shape. She seems to be frozen in shock.

GULP!

A bride can't wear a dress with blue paint on it, can she? My mind begins to race with ideas. Maybe we can borrow a dress from Mommy. Or hide it by decorating it with flowers.

My heart is hammering in my chest. If only Jakey had washed his hands.

Jakey looks sheepish as he waits at the bathroom door.

"Don't tell me that you are thinking of locking her in there again," I warn him. "We can't kidnap the bride from her own wedding!"

"I'm sorry," he says, sniffing. "I promise I'll wash my hands next time! I didn't mean to ruin her dress."

The toilet flushes and Annie comes out smiling. Jakey leads me away.

"She hasn't seen the paint," he whispers in astonishment.

"She must be too nervous to notice," I marvel.

"I couldn't help it. I was just so excited to see her," he says, sniffing again, looking regretfully down at his blue hands.

Now Mommy rushes in. "The guests are seated," she tells us, smiling at Annie. Luckily for us she hasn't spotted the blue paint either.

I hear the organ begin to play "Here Comes the Bride."

What should I do? A part of me thinks that I should tell Annie, because walking down the aisle with blue handprints on her bottom would be embarrassing, but another part of me thinks of what Dad always says: "What you don't know can't hurt you."

So I get my flower basket and brush my hair. As we all head into the hall, I suddenly

remember number three on Mommy's list.
I am the ring bearer!

I race back to the windowsill, but would
you believe it? The gold rings and their pillow
are GONE. I am panicking. My stomach is
churning like a washing machine. I look . . .

UNDER the chairs,

BEHIND the curtains,

IN the bathroom,

. . . but I can't find the rings anywhere.
I have lost them!

It's nearly time for Annie to walk down the aisle. Jakey and I are supposed to walk in front of her. But I am in the back room looking for the rings!

I feel tears coming. There is only one person who can help—Marge. She is standing in the doorway, watching me race around. She seems worried too. I am about to cry.

"Marge," I say in panic, "I lost the rings!"

"Jemima," Marge confesses, her rainbow-wave hairstyle beginning to droop sadly, "I lost baby Zara!"

Well, I don't need to be a detective to work out this puzzle. Baby Zara has stolen the rings and run away! Everyone knows that pirate babies love trinkets. I am sure if we find that one-fanged baby thief, we will find those rings. We dash about madly looking for Zara, but she is nowhere to be seen.

Marge heads outside as I run all the way to the back of the hall to find Jakey. Maybe my little brother can help us. Just as I arrive, the organ song gets even louder as if it's telling us to hurry up.

"We have to go NOW!" Jakey tells me.

He grabs my hand and drags me forward. We are going to lead the procession; that's what flower girls and ring bearers do.

At the back of the grand room, Annie is standing with her father. Mommy waves at us proudly from her seat. She nods at me to signal that it's time to set off, just as we practiced. I take a deep breath and try to think calm thoughts. Slowly Jakey and I start walking down the aisle in time to the music.

All I can see are lots of faces and weird lady hats, but then I see Granny and Grandpa,

so I wave to them. Jakey spots Theo and Matthew's dad in a pin-striped suit. Before we know it, we have finished the walk. Together we turn back to face everyone and smile as big as the moon and do jazz hands, just like Marge told us to.

Annie is also smiling from the back of the room. She looks like a princess in her pearly puffy wedding dress.

Uncle Desmond's eyes are so happy.

But I am still scared. My heart is pounding in my ears. What will happen when they ask me for the rings? I can't believe Jakey and I have ruined Annie's big day.

I am so full of my own thoughts, I barely notice people whispering and nudging each other. But as Annie walks up the aisle, the sounds grow louder. Then I see people snickering and hiding their snorts of laughter behind their hands. Lucy's Mommy and Mabel look perplexed. What is going on? Even Dad is frowning in confusion.

Now I see why.

Walking behind Annie as she glides down the aisle, oblivious to the giggles, is tiny Marge. And she is holding her paintbrush! She is dabbing the back of the bride's wedding dress with the magic green goo potion that removes paint.

What a good idea, Marge!

Luckily, Annie is too happy to notice, and before they reach the front, Marge ducks behind a pillar.

Annie stands and faces her husband-to-be, looking radiant. Her dress is white again, the blue handprints completely gone.

Jakey nudges me. Because we are very close, I can see a tiny damp patch on Annie's dress where the creamy satin has turned see-through. Jake and I can see Annie's underwear!

He whispers to me: "Annie Alligator just became Annie Underpants!"

For the first time I forget about the missing rings. In fact I nearly collapse in giggles, but then I see Mommy looking at us and I stand nicely. I turn my body away from Jakey because I must not laugh.

Now the justice of the peace is talking. He has a mustache that twitches when he speaks.

I really hope he doesn't get angry at me in front of everyone when he realizes that I have lost the rings.

"Do you, Desmond Button, take Annie Nutley to be your partner in life, to love and cherish through good times and bad?"

My uncle says, "I do," and smiles at Annie.

While everyone gazes happily at the couple, I turn around and sneak a peek for Marge. And I spy her whizzing across the back of the hall as fast as her short legs can carry her!

The justice of the peace turns to Annie Underpants and says, "Do you, Annie Nutley, take Desmond Button to be your partner in life, for richer and poorer?"

I pretend to scratch my neck so I can turn around again. This time I glimpse Marge running in the other direction.

"I do," Annie says as she gazes into my uncle's eyes. I can see that they are very much in love. I can't wait to be a bride one day.

"Who is the ring bearer?" the justice of the peace asks, looking in my direction.

I don't know what to do, so I stare at my shoes and gulp.

Everyone is looking around, and the justice of the peace clears his throat. "Where are the rings? Who has them?" he asks again.

My face grows hot and red. Jakey nudges me, and I can see Mommy is staring at me too.

"Grrrrr!" growls a voice loudly behind us.

Zara is holding the ring pillow as she speeds down the aisle with Marge in hot pursuit.

PHEW

"THAT SMALL BUT DANGEROUS PIRATE stole the rings!" Jakey shouts in his outdoor voice, whipping his plastic sword out of his pants and pointing it at Zara.

The justice of the peace looks surprised.

Everyone's eyes are now on Zara.

She pauses and gives an adorable smile while trying to find an escape route.

Now Archie bolts down the aisle.

WOOF
WOOF

Mommy's face is beginning to go as green as Marge's magic potion. Our puppy gallops past Dad, who tries to catch him but misses. Archie bounds over to Zara and grabs the ring pillow in his jaws.

"Wait, is *that* the ring bearer?" The justice of the peace looks confused as he points to our puppy.

"No, that's our muse," Jakey corrects him.

"Walkies," I call, and Archie trots toward me. I reach out and grab the pillow just as Marge scoops Zara into her arms and vanishes out of the hall.

"I am the ring bearer." I grin triumphantly, holding up two gold wedding bands.

Everyone in the hall is now on their feet, cheering and clapping like it's a concert!

"ARGH-HAA!" I can hear Zara's piratey voice in the distance.

Eventually all the grown-ups settle down. I have never been as relieved in my life as when I hand over the rings to the justice of the peace.

"Is there anyone here who knows any reason that these two people should not be married? If so, please speak up now."

Everyone is silent, and I look out at my mommy and dad, who both have happy tears sliding down their faces. Grandpa and Granny are holding hands, and Aunt Sally and Uncle Nick are sharing a smile. Just when I am thinking that the wedding is now going very smoothly, my little brother stands up.

"I HAVE A REASON," announces Jakey in his outdoor voice.

Instantly the room is absolutely silent.

Everyone is looking at Jakey, at both of us. What is he going to say?

The justice of the peace looks confused. "Go on—what is the reason?" he asks.

"She looks like a marshmallow!" Jakey jokes, pointing at Annie. Oh no, Jakey has broken Mommy's rule number six about staying quiet during the service.

Everyone gasps in surprise . . . but luckily Annie throws back her head and laughs and laughs. And then the whole hall joins in! Mommy and Uncle Desmond and everyone—even the justice of the peace—are chuckling and smiling and giggling. Dear old Mabel nearly rolls out into the aisle. Mrs. Beacher knocks her own hat off, she is laughing so hard.

Once everyone has settled down again, the justice of the peace puts his hand on the shoulders of Annie and Uncle Desmond. "Finally . . . you may kiss the bride!"

He wipes his brow and sighs with relief.

Uncle Desmond takes Annie Underpants's face in his hands and kisses her gently.

I whisper to Jakey that we can throw our rose petals now.

Everyone cheers as we sprinkle the bride and groom, but suddenly we hear . . .

"OW!"

"STOP!!"

"OUCH!"

Jakey is throwing the hard mint candies that he sneaked from the bowl earlier. They're raining down on the bride and groom like little stones!

"Sorry—I ran out of petals," Jakey explains.

He scampers around picking up the mints and trying to eat them until Mommy pulls him away. Poor Jakey cannot control himself when he gets excited.

Right after that we get to go into another grand room, with twinkly lights on the ceiling. There are lots of white tables and chairs and a chocolate fountain and a band. Marge explains that if we get split up, we have to meet back at the chocolate fountain for a midnight swim.

Jakey, Marge, Archie, and I have the best time (once Jakey has taken off his itchy tie and baby Zara has fallen asleep in her carriage). We crawl around beneath the tables while the boring speeches are happening, and then we sneak three giant slices of cake under there and have a picnic.

As we devour the yummy food, Marge entertains us with stories of the Duchess of Winkerstink's wedding extravaganza.

When the band starts playing, it's too loud for us to hear each other, so we all boogie. I am doing silly star jumps with Mommy until Dad lets me dance with him, standing on his feet.

Jakey, Theo, and Matthew look like kangaroos doing karate as they hop and chop the air.

And Marge and Archie are doing the tango.

It's the best party I have ever been to. And the only time I have ever seen grown-ups having so much fun. Later on we sneak out to Uncle Desmond's car and start covering it with our decorations. I put streamers on the roof and we all throw confetti and stick our pictures on the dashboard. Jakey puts the rest of his candies on the front seat. You should see Annie Underpants's and Desmond's faces when they spot their car. They look so happy!

Although Uncle Desmond's face is a little less happy when he sits down on the hard candies.

Ouch!

But no one is annoyed with my little brother. He has helped to make their wedding day extraspecial. And even though we made a few mistakes, I think that being a flower girl has been the best job ever. I can't wait to get married when I grow up.

I'm sure you're wondering if we ever swam in the chocolate fountain. Well, I am not going to answer that in case Mommy and Dad read this story, but let's just say . . . I still have chocolate behind my ears!

Read on for a sneak peek at

Marge in Charge and the Missing Orangutan!

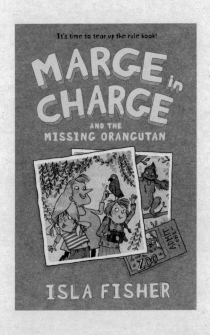

"COME OUT!" I say.

My four-year-old brother is hiding under his bed.

"Marge is here!" I am so happy.

Marge, the best babysitter in the whole universe, is at our house, and my little brother doesn't care. I don't know what is wrong with him. Marge is not like a normal, boring babysitter. Marge is just the opposite: she is a member of the royal family, and she once helped us build a dinosaur out of pancakes.

Mommy and Dad appear in the doorway looking sharp. Dad is in a suit and Mommy is wearing a fancy black shirt.

"We have to leave for the party now. Please come out," Dad begs.

"NO!" Jakey sounds mad. This is not like him at all. Usually when he hears that Marge is coming, he pulls his shorts over his head like a wrestling mask and races to the door to greet her.

I walk with our parents to the hallway where Marge is waiting. I always forget how small she is. Even though I am only seven years old, I am nearly as tall as our grown-up babysitter. She can even fit inside our play tent without bending over.

Today she is wearing a shiny silver shirt and a strange silver hat.

"Greetings, earthling," Marge jokes, giving me a robotic wave. She does look a little like she has come from outer space, and I giggle.

"We won't be back until late." Dad gives me a hug. "And remember, Marge is in charge!"

"See if you can cheer Jakey up," Mommy says as she grabs her car keys. "He's been under that bed since he got home from school." Then, as she is half out the door, she remembers. "I left the rules on the fridge."

Usually Marge adds things to Mommy's rules to make them more fun, like the time when she took us to Theo's birthday party. Marge changed Mommy's rule about only eating one slice of cake at the party to *nine* slices!!

The minute we have waved off our old blue car, Marge does my favorite thing. She takes off her hat and shakes out her long rainbow hair. It is so crazy—red, green, yellow, orange, and blue.

"Let's go cheer up your brother!" Marge dances down the corridor and into our bedroom. I am getting very mad at Jakey; it's so exciting to have Marge here, and all he is doing is hiding and ruining the fun.

I want Marge to tell us wild stories about
when she lived in the palace or traveled the
world with her fourteen pets.

"Jakey?" Marge pretends she can't see his
legs poking out from underneath the bed.

"Yoo-hoo," she calls, checking behind the
curtains and inside my closet.

"Where are youuuuuu?" she sings.

"I'm under here," a little voice replies.

Marge hoists up her skirt and crawls under his bed. I wriggle in after her until we are both facing Jakey.

My brother's face is blotchy and red.

"Whatever is the matter?" Marge asks. "I haven't seen such a sad face since the marquis of Humperdink played tennis in the ballroom and smashed his favorite Ming vase."

"My tooth won't come out." Jakey's bottom lip is quivering. "I've had this stupid wobbly tooth for so long and it won't budge!"

"That is terrible news." Marge looks grave.

"Theo lost a tooth and the tooth fairy gave him a whole quarter!" Theo has one long eyebrow and is Jakey's best friend from school.

"The tooth fairy is never going to visit me," Jakey whimpers.

"Never say never, Jakeypants," Marge tells him. "I remember when I thought I was never going to see my hairy-nosed wombat, George, again after he buried himself underneath the castle moat, but then, one day, there he was! Sunning himself on the queen's lounge chair, drinking tea and wearing her missing tiara."

Marge shuffles closer to Jakey. "Can I see?" She gently wobbles his tooth with her finger.

"I've tried pulling it out," Jakey says, sniffing. "I've wiggled and pushed, but it's stuck."

"Dentist Marge to the rescue!" Marge exclaims, and at last Jakey smiles. "All we need is your dad's tool kit."

The smile runs away from my little brother's face, and he looks a little frightened as we all crawl backward out from under the bed.

Then Marge tells me that I will be the dental assistant, which I am actually quite excited about.

"I once removed my Persian cat Amelia's left fang, after she broke into the palace pantry and ate too many candies. It was rotten to the core!" Marge tells Jakey. "I also pulled a tooth that had been stuck in a suit of armor in the castle for a thousand years. The knight didn't feel a thing!"

I run to the garage and come back with Dad's toolbox and Marge whistles as she searches through it. I have the brilliant idea that we might need protective gear in case there is blood, so I grab an apron from the kitchen.

"Lie down," I tell Jakey as Marge puts on a gigantic pair of goggles.

'Open up! WIDE.'

Hilarious books by
ISLA FISHER

Everything is way more fun
when Marge is in charge!

HARPER

An Imprint of HarperCollinsPublishers

www.harpercollinschildrens.com